Dreaming book
and being …..
ein Buch zum Nachdenken
und lachen

Impressum:

Bibliografische Information der Deutschen Nationalbibliothek: Die Deutsche Nationalbibliothek verzeichnet diese Publikation in der Deutschen Nationalbibliografie; detaillierte bibliografische Daten sind im Internet über www.dnb.de abrufbar.

© 2020 Peter Oberfrank – Hunziker
Herstellung und Verlag
BoD – Books on Demand, Norderstedt

ISBN 9783734773945

Dieses Buch ist ganz kreativ und träumen bedeutet auch schönes sein und die Natur ist wunderschön. Sportliches sein ist auch großartig und zauberhaft und auch zu reisen ist beeindruckend und das Zuhause ist märchenhaft schön und herzlich. Eine bunte Welt ist ein netter Ausdruck und dieses Buch ist tiefsinnig und bietet auch Platz zum selber schreiben und zeichnen in diesem Buch.

Yipiyeah …..

Rapperswil

Indianerblumenland city

Garmisch

New York

Chicago

Region Germany

Herzidorf in Schweiz

Hamburg

Bremen

Anaheim

Dallas

Las Vegas

Arizona

Florida

Montreal

Toronto

Calgary

Minnesota

Salt Lake City

Los Angeles

Colorado

Columbus

Moskau

KAC Dorf

Detroit

New Yersey

Philadelphia

San Jose

Buffalo

New York Island

St. Louis

Washington

Edmonton

Winnipeg

Carolina

San Francisco

Yuttah

Mexiko city

Buenos Aires

Rio de Janeiro

Texas city

Dschungel city

Vancouver

Tampa Bay

Nashville

Lorenzo city

Watersprings city

Boston

Ottawa

Pittsburgh

AJK dorfi

Doha

Australien city

Köln

asian

Homburg

San Antonio

Frankfurt

asiati city town

alpine city Innsbruck

Zürich

Rosenheim

Chiemsee city

Berlin

Oslo

Stockholm

Helsinki

Reykjavik

Nordpol city

Afrika city

Kapstadt

Blumengo

Südpol city

Dschungel town

Dehli

Afrikanis

Asien

Indien

Rom

Neapel

Gardasee city

Verona

Turin

Mailand

Cesenatico

Luruna

Paris

Barcelona

Madrid

Valencia

Lissabon

Baumiland city

Sizilien

Venezuela city

Hawai

Miami

Woodilandcity

Homburg dorfi

Glücklichkeitsdorf

Swissi

Lago di Garda in Amerika

Lake Louise

Red heart village

Green heart village

cosy town

Colour town

New Zealand

Dubai

Ägypten

Weissensee city

Villach

Graz

Klagenfurt

Wien

Dubrovsk

Niagaraland City

siberia city

Luzern city

Hampshire

Melbourne

floweriland

Hollywood town

Santa Monica beach city

Israel city

Athenes

Burundi

Holland city

Venezia

Curun city

Rosen city

Brüssel

Butswanalongo city

Herz city

sporty town city

Angabe zum gezeichneten Originalbild
am Buchcover:

Indianerblumenland, gezeichnet von
Peter Oberfrank – Hunziker im Jahr
2020 mit Buntstiften am Papier